EVANS JR HIGH SCHOOL

P9-APC-842

201014316   FIC SPA

Dog walker

DATE DUE

Demco, Inc. 38-293

Dog Walker

Karen Spafford-Fitz

Orca currents

ORCA BOOK PUBLISHERS

*For Ken and Dornoch whose friendship inspired this story
and for Anna and Shannon who inspire me daily.*

Library and Archives Canada Cataloguing in Publication

Spafford-Fitz, Karen, 1963-
Dog walker / Karen Spafford-Fitz.
(Orca currents)

ISBN 10: 1-55143-533-0 (bound) ISBN 10: 1-55143-522-5 (pbk.)
ISBN 13: 978-1-55143-533-6 (bound) ISBN 13: 978-1-55143-522-0 (pbk.)

I. Title. II. Series.
PS8637.P33D63 2006   JC813'.6   C2006-900467-6

First published in the United States, 2006
Library of Congress Control Number: 2006921146

Summary: Turk's moneymaking scheme gets out of control.

Orca Book Publishers gratefully acknowledges the support for its publishing
programs provided by the following agencies: the Government of Canada
through the Canada Book Fund and the Canada Council for the Arts,
and the Province of British Columbia through the BC Arts Council
and the Book Publishing Tax Credit.

Cover design by Lynn O'Rourke
Cover photography by Getty Images

ORCA BOOK PUBLISHERS
PO Box 5626, Stn. B
Victoria, BC Canada
V8R 6S4

ORCA BOOK PUBLISHERS
PO Box 468
Custer, WA USA
98240-0468

www.orcabook.com
Printed and bound in Canada.
Printed on 100% PCW recycled paper.

13 12 11 10 • 6 5 4 3

chapter one

What Your Teen is Really Feeling. Supporting Your Child's Interests. Enjoying Quality Family Time Together. Those are some of the headlines I've seen in Mom's parenting magazines. The one about quality family time is really messing with my life.

Here's how it goes: The magazine arrives in the mail, then Mom gets weird and thoughtful for a few days. The next thing I know, she schedules quality family time.

Attendance mandatory. First she dragged Dad and me through a bunch of art galleries. Then we had to go out for dinner at a fancy restaurant that didn't even have pizza on the menu. Last month she made me play golf at her and Dad's private golf club. Which brings me to tonight—spending Friday night playing a lame board game at home with my parents. I don't have tons of other options. But still, this sucks.

"How do you feel about the game?" Mom asks as she hands me two hundred dollars of Monopoly money for passing Go.

"Sad," I say.

Mom looks pleased. She thinks she just scored big points in the parenting world for getting me to *open up about my feelings* while *sharing some good, old-fashioned fun.*

"Really? What do you find sad about it?"

That's when I stick it to her. "Those dollar bills you're handing me? They won't buy me a *thing*!"

Mom's jaw drops. "What do you mean, Turk? You could buy a railroad."

"Yeah, Mom. That's the dream of every

fourteen-year-old guy. To buy a fake railroad with fake money on a Friday night."

"I get the message, Turk," Mom says through gritted teeth. "In other words, you don't appreciate that I picked up a nice new Monopoly game. Or that I planned a lovely night at home together."

"It sure wasn't my choice," I shrug. Then I hold up my wad of Monopoly money. "You've got to admit, Dad, if this was *real* cash, it might be worth getting excited about."

Dad chuckles. Then he catches himself.

Mom's cheeks turn red and blotchy. This is usually a sign for me to shut up. I've learned from bitter experience that if you tick Mom off, it always catches up with you. But it's like I have a death wish tonight.

"In fact," I say, "why don't you put me in charge of family nights? If you slipped me some money, I'd take care of everything. Then we'll have some real fun! And who knows? I might even have some money left over for myself. Enough dough to update my stereo system. Or upgrade the options on

3

my cell phone. Now *that's* exciting! As for playing a few rounds of Monopoly..."

"Quite frankly, Turk, I doubt you could do any of those things—even if this *were* real money!" Mom flings her Monopoly money down onto the table. "Not with how quickly you burn through your allowance." Mom's voice is getting higher with every word. I swear her nostrils are flaring too.

"So what if I ask for the occasional loan? What's the big deal?"

"The big deal is that it's not just occasionally. You apparently don't appreciate how lucky you are. And you certainly don't help out around here in return."

"You've gotta be kidding!" I say. "You mean work? You know I don't believe in breaking a sweat." I shudder.

"Yes, your imaginary allergy," Mom says.

"Hey, can I help it if I'm allergic to my own sweat?" I laugh.

Mom stands up and pushes her chair back—hard. "You two can count your fake money together. I'll go get the snacks."

Dad springs from the loveseat. "Let me help you, honey."

Good kissing up, Dad. That must be how you landed the vice president's job.

From the lounger, I can hear Mom chewing Dad out at top speed in the kitchen. Dad's agreeing with her nearly as fast.

When they come out a few minutes later, Mom is carrying a plate of smoked salmon and crackers. Dad has two glasses of champagne and a glass of iced tea on a tray. Apparently none of Mom's parenting magazines mention that teenagers like pizza and Coke for snacks. Or that popcorn works too.

Mom still looks pretty ticked, so I don't say anything about her choice of snacks.

She turns to Dad. "Mack, I think *you* should tell *your* son why he needs to manage his money better."

Dad chews his smoked salmon slowly, like a man who's on death row. "It's like this...er, Turk..."

Just then, the doorbell rings.

"Saved by the bell," I laugh.

Mom stomps off to the front door. Then she does that thing that always blows me away. In the blink of an eye, she switches into her favorite role: the vice president's wife.

As she opens the door, Mom sings out, "*Loretta!* Goodness, *Loretta!* How delightful to see you!"

Loretta. The president's wife.

I picture Mom planting pretend kisses into the air on both sides of Loretta's plump cheeks.

Then I hear something else. *Yap! Yap! Yip!*

"Loretta," Mom says, "I haven't met your little friend."

"This is Gretzky," Loretta yells over more puppy yips. "She's a cockapoo. A *female* cockapoo. But Vincent insisted on naming her Gretzky. My dear husband never got over Wayne Gretzky leaving Edmonton."

Loretta and *a yapping puppy! I'm out of here!*

But there's no escape. Loretta has just flung herself into the living room in a cloud of flowery perfume. Gretzky, a yapping coffee-colored hairball, is nestled against the lavender frills on Loretta's enormous chest.

"Hello, Turkingtons," Loretta blares.

At that moment, Gretzky leaps from Loretta's arms and bounces into my lap.

"You want a little playsy-waysy with Winston, do you?" Loretta says with a tinkly laugh.

I cringe. Winston is my real name and I can't stand it. So everyone—except Loretta, that is—calls me Turk. It's short for my last name, Turkington.

"Sorry. I'm on my way to bed. I'm all playsy-waysied out for today." I try to nudge Gretzky off my lap. No luck.

From the corner of my eye, I catch Mom's warning look.

"Look at how frisky she is now that she's found a new playmate," Loretta gushes.

"Playmate? Me?" I say.

"Why yes." Loretta turns to Mom. "Remember when I told you I was getting a puppy? You told me that you and Winston love puppies. You said you were considering getting a puppy yourself."

"News to me," I mutter.

I've never stopped to think about whether I like dogs or not. But if I did, I'd probably decide they're okay, but only at a distance. And as for this hairball that's yapping like crazy on my lap—

"*Gross!*"

She licks my chin again. What if she just drank from the toilet? And I swear, if she tries to sniff my crotch—

"And that you'd love to help out with Gretzky any time at all," Loretta says.

"Why...why, yes. I mean, I...suppose I *might* have said something like that."

Why won't this dog get off me?

"Vincent and I are heading out of town," Loretta continues. "Just this morning, I took Gretzky to a kennel that I'd heard wonderful things about. But I took one look at those— those *cages*—and I couldn't leave my baby there. Then I remembered your kind offer. And now to see Gretzky so happy here with Winston—well, I know I did the right thing."

As I try to swish Gretzky off my lap again,

I glance at Mom. Her face has a serious cramp in it.

"Here's Gretzky's water dish and her little supper bowl." Loretta pulls two fancy bowls out of her enormous flowered bag.

"And here's her favorite little stuffy-toy for bedtime." It might be a teddy bear, but it's hard to tell. One leg and most of its face are chewed off.

Dad, who's paralyzed in the loveseat, reaches for more smoked salmon. At that very moment, Gretzky launches herself onto the coffee table and polishes off the rest of the salmon. Dad clears his throat and sits back.

"And here's Gretzky's favorite dog food. And let's see what else..." She pulls out a flowered cushion and a pink baby blanket.

"Gretzky likes to sleep on her mommy's bed. I'm sure you and Mack won't mind."

Mom's face cramps up even tighter. I try to imagine a dog sleeping on her expensive new duvet.

Loretta gazes down at Gretzky. "Mommy's going to miss her little sweetheart." Her eyes well up with tears as she crouches down and plants a kiss on Gretzky's head. Gretzky is too busy tugging on Mom's Persian rug to notice.

Mom finally squeaks out a few words. "How long are you going for?"

"Just for the weekend. We'll be home Sunday evening."

Mom cheers up a bit. "I'm sure we can, er...manage Gretzky until then."

"Toodle-oo!" Loretta vanishes in a lavender poof out the door.

I look at Gretzky. The edge of Mom's rug still dangles from between her teeth. Then I remember Mom's blow-up about the Monopoly game and a really bad feeling creeps into my gut. Mom must be ticking like a time bomb now. Time to make myself scarce.

I'm bolting up to my bedroom when a bloodcurdling scream pierces the air.

"No, Gretzky. *Stop!*" Mom shrieks. "Mack, she just *peed* on the Persian rug!"

Faster than a hyper puppy lunging for a plate of smoked salmon, I dash into my bedroom. I lock the door behind me just in case!

chapter two

Sleeping is what I do best, especially on the weekend. I can sleep through thunderstorms. I can sleep while the cleaning lady vacuums. I can sleep while a new roof is being hammered on. But I learned last night that I can't sleep with Gretzky in the house.

Here's how it went:

Gretzky yapping at two in the morning.

Gretzky howling at four-thirty in the morning.

Gretzky whining just before six o'clock.

And my favorite: Gretzky yodeling around seven o'clock.

Mom and Dad's reactions hardly lulled me back to sleep either. At first they tried speaking kindly to her. Then came the warnings about waking up the whole house, as if Gretzky cared, and as if we weren't all awake anyway. Next came the threats.

"Gretzky! Another peep out of you and there'll be no more smoked salmon!"

So it's almost noon before I crawl out of bed and pull on some clothes.

On the way downstairs, I call Leo on my cell phone.

"Hey, Leo."

"Turk?"

"Still meeting at Starbucks?"

"Yeah." We meet for hot chocolate every Saturday afternoon.

As I step down from the last stair, Gretzky yaps louder than ever.

"What's that?" Leo asks.

"A cockapoo."

"A what-a-poo?"

"A yapping hairball, okay? I'll explain later. See you in ten minutes."

I take one look at Mom and Dad's tired faces and I know this is not where I want to be. Time to exit the house. Fast.

I veer toward the front door with Gretzky yapping at my feet.

I'm almost there when Mom speaks up. "Freeze!"

"What?"

"I said 'freeze.'"

"Why?"

"Gretzky."

Yap!

"What about her?"

"Your dad and I have been on Gretzky-duty all night."

I'm not sure where this is going, but I don't like it.

"Now it's your turn." Mom pauses to pull a wet stringy piece of her Persian rug out of Gretzky's mouth. "Besides, looking after Gretzky will give you something responsible to do. Who knows? You might even—how did you put it last night?—break a sweat."

So that's what this is about. Payback time.

I definitely need to get out of here.

But then I remember I don't have any money! I'd better soften Mom up a bit before I ask for next month's allowance. Or am I up to the month after that?

"Sounds like you guys didn't get much sleep last night either. Pretty rough, wasn't it? Especially for a growing boy. Wasn't there something in one of your parenting magazines, Mom, about how teenagers don't get enough sleep these days?"

I shake my head and try to look serious. I can't tell if Mom's buying it or not.

"But listen," I say. "I've gotta go meet Leo at Starbucks. Could you spare me some cash?"

Mom glares at me.

"For a hot chocolate." Still nothing.

"I can't think of one good reason why I should hand you a dime."

"Here's a good reason: Leo picked up the

tab the last three weeks in a row. Doesn't that make you feel ashamed?"

"No. Get a job."

"A what?"

"A job," Mom says. "You're not getting another cent out of your father and me. And, you're not going anywhere. Unless," her face takes on an evil glow, "Gretzky goes with you."

Gretzky is tugging at my shoelaces and doing a fake puppy snarl.

"Take Gretzky for a *walk?*"

Mom nods.

"But—"

"Here's her leash." Mom shoves it into my hands. Gretzky drops my shoelaces. She yips loudly as she jumps up and grabs at her leash.

"Don't forget to take some plastic bags with you."

"What for?"

"In case Gretzky needs the potty when you're out walking together. Also known as 'going number two.'"

"I have to pick it up?"

"You can't just leave it there."

"I can't?"

Mom reaches down and snaps Gretzky's leash onto her collar. "Now get outside. Both of you." Mom stuffs some plastic bags into my hand. "We're going back to bed. Don't hurry home."

I stumble toward the front door, trying not to step on the bouncing hairball beside me.

I'm halfway to Starbucks before I realize that Mom pulled a quick one on me. She sent me out the door without handing over any cash.

My future flashes before me. A yapping cockapoo for a social life. Sweating it out scooping up dog poop. And broke too.

chapter three

I'm peering through the front window of
Starbucks when the door opens.

"Oh my *God*! That is the cutest puppy
I've ever seen!"

"What?" I turn around. I can't believe my
eyes. The girl talking to me is *beautiful*!

She flicks her long red hair back from her
face. "Aren't you just a little sweetie," she
gushes as she stoops to pat Gretzky.

Gretzky drops to the ground in front of the girl.

I search for something intelligent to say. Even something mildly stupid would be better than nothing.

"Excuse me," a different voice says from behind me.

I turn to see an elderly woman who's pulling a little cart. "You're blocking the doorway."

"Sorry."

"That's okay." The woman's face lights up. "You two look so lovely together."

At first I think the woman is talking about Gretzky and me. Then I realize she means this great-looking girl and me. I blush bright red.

"I'd better be on my way," the woman says, pulling the cart behind her.

"Me too," the girl says, standing up.

With a final pat on Gretzky's head, she smiles and bounces away.

"How did you manage that?"

I jump and turn around.

"The girl, Turk," says Leo. "Why was she

talking to *you*? Did you knock her over or something?"

"Very funny."

Gretzky yips beside me.

"What's that?" Leo points at Gretzky.

"Gretzky. The cockapoo I told you about. She belongs to Loretta, this woman that Mom knows. Loretta's husband is Dad's boss."

"I get it. Someone you've gotta impress, right?"

"Right. We're looking after Gretzky for her this weekend."

"Lucky you." Then Leo catches himself. "I mean—I don't hate dogs or anything. It's just that they do some gross stuff. You know, like smelling each other's butts."

I decide not to tell Leo why I have plastic bags wadded up in my pocket.

Instead I say, "Yeah, and too bad they're not allowed in coffee shops. So Leo, do you mind?"

"You expect me to fall for that?"

"What?"

"Who bought the hot chocolates last week? And the week before that?"

"But Leo, I'm out of cash."

"Again? Ask your parents for some. They've got loads of dough."

"Truth is, Leo, they're ticked off at me."

"What for this time?"

"A few comments I made. About the Monopoly game last night."

"Monopoly? Don't tell me. More quality family time?"

"You got it. Nothing I'd rather be doing. Not that I have any better options. Not with my thrilling life, you know."

"I hear you." Leo nods.

Then we both get quiet. Leo's probably thinking about the same thing I am: the big zero of our social lives. Neither Leo, nor me, nor the rest of our friends can figure it out. Sure, we're kind of skinny and shy. And we don't attract girls like those athletic guys do. You know, the types who score dates with girls even faster than they score points for their hockey and basketball teams. But still, it's not like there's anything *wrong* with us either.

The only way we even have the tiniest social life is by a total fluke. Leo's cousin,

Meghan, is one of the popular in-demand girls at school. She is always touching up her makeup at her locker or sorting out her complicated social life over the cell phone that's permanently glued to her ear. Along with her best friend, Lexia, Meghan occasionally takes pity on Leo and me and invites us along for a Coke or something.

"Okay, okay," Leo says. "I'll get the drinks."

Leo turns back before he steps into the coffee shop. "How about getting a job, man?"

"Not you too!" I say, thinking back to Mom's words.

Suddenly Gretzky yaps and tugs at her leash.

"What a little *sweetheart!* Can I pat your puppy?"

"Uh, sure."

I fix my eyes on the girl in front of me. Her blond hair bounces as she reaches to rub Gretzky's chin. "Oh, you little darling. You like this, don't you?"

Yeah, what's not to like!

But just like before, I can't think of anything to say.

"What's his name?"

"Uh, Gretzky."

"Gretzky? Like the hockey player?"

"Yeah."

"Well, he's gorgeous."

"Uh, yeah. Only it's not a boy dog. More like...uh...a girl."

"Oh. I didn't notice." She blushes in a shade of pink that matches her lipstick. "Cute. Gretzky the girl. I like that."

I nod dumbly.

"Hello, Gretzky Girl." She shakes Gretzky's paw. "I'm Mallory. How do you do?"

Just then, Leo steps out of the coffee shop.

"Here you go, Turk." At the sight of Mallory, Leo pulls his hand away. "I don't think we've met."

Like me and the rest of our friends, Leo fails miserably in the girlfriend department. But that doesn't stop him from being totally girl crazy. And at least he can think of something to say. Unlike me.

"I'm Mallory," she says.

"Hi, Mallory. I'm Leo."

"Oh, hi." Mallory glances at her watch. "Sorry, but I've gotta go." She looks down at Gretzky again. "Bye, Gretzky Girl."

"Just when I was getting somewhere—maybe." Leo shakes his head sadly as she walks away. "By the way, Turk, how did you manage that?"

"What?"

"Girls who look like *that* never talk to you."

"They do today."

"Oh yeah," Leo says. "That other girl too." He looks confused. "What's going on?"

"Beats me."

Then the answer comes to me in a rush. Or rather, in a yip.

Yip, yip, yip.

"Gretzky!"

"That's it, man. It's the furball that girls are falling for, Turk. Not you." Leo laughs. "I shoulda known."

I'm just about to remind Leo of all the times he's struck out too when something starts to gel in my mind.

Suddenly an idea is born. Right outside of Starbucks on Whyte Avenue.

"Leo, man. I'm onto something."

"What?"

"I'm going to start a new business. My money problems are over. I'm going to be rolling in dough. And you and the rest of the guys are going to be rolling in girlfriends."

Leo's eyes nearly pop out of his head.

Before he can ask me anything, I say, "Wait for me at your locker tomorrow after school. I'll fill you in then. Tell all the other guys to be there too."

Leo whistles softly under his breath. "We'll be there all right."

My future doesn't look so grim anymore. Except for when Gretzky goes number two and I have to scoop it into a plastic bag, I smile all the way home.

chapter four

By Monday morning, I'm so eager to start my business that I hardly notice anything. Or anyone.

"Move over, Turk."

"Sorry, Carly."

I close my locker partway so Carly can open hers beside me. Carly moved to my school back in grade four. For some reason, she loves running. She trains a lot with a running club, and she enters a lot of races.

I don't get that—especially with all the hard work and sweating that goes with it. But anyway, Carly's last name, Turnbull, is close to Turkington. So our coat hooks were side by side in elementary school. Now our lockers are side by side in junior high too. That's the good news.

The bad news is there's someone else whose last name is also close to mine: Turcotte. Chuck Turcotte. Or "Upchuck" Turcotte, as most of us call him. Not that he's smart enough to notice. And speaking of sweating, Chuck does more than enough sweating for both him and me.

"What's up, loser? Hey, move over." Chuck gives me a shove. Any chance to flex his big stupid muscles makes Chuck really happy.

"Hey, Upchuck," I say, trying not to look shaken.

"Hey, buddy," Chuck bellows. "I'm just playing with you a bit. But you don't mind, right?"

I know what's coming next. Chuck is going to start acting like we're best buddies.

This is even worse than when he's showing off his brute strength.

He claps his arm over my shoulder. Unfortunately Chuck is way taller than all the grade nine guys, including me. So my face is about level with his yellow armpit stain. The smell of his stinky armpit and cheap aftershave hits me square in the face. Beside me, Carly makes a gagging sound.

"You gotta get yourself to a gym, Stick Man," Chuck bellows out. "Do something about that scrawny build of yours."

I shrug his arm off my shoulder and take a step back. "I like my scrawny build just the way it is," I say.

Chuck laughs. "Then I guess you haven't checked out *these* biceps lately."

I glance over at Chuck who is admiring his biceps in the mirror he has hanging in his locker. Carly snickers. I roll my eyes. Chuck, meanwhile, is flexing hard.

"Careful, man," I say. "You might hurt yourself."

"Hey, don't worry about *me*." I take another step back. For some reason, Chuck can't talk to anyone without being right in their face. And he also sprays about a jug full of spit at you in the process.

Something shifts in Chuck's locker. He swears and tries to grab everything before it falls, but he doesn't move fast enough. A pile of bodybuilding magazines slides onto the floor. A mountain of dirty gym clothes tumbles down after them.

"Jeez, Chuck! You've gotta wash that stuff!"

"Or burn it," Carly says.

Chuck stuffs everything back in.

"Are you saving those sweaty T-shirts for trophies or something?"

"Don't worry about those, little man," Chuck says. "Pump some iron, and you might fit into one of ol' Chuck's T-shirts yourself some day."

I nearly gag at the thought. And it doesn't help that Chuck is now stuffing his face with a disgusting-looking green energy bar.

"Can't get enough protein into me these days." Bits of energy bar are spraying out of Chuck's mouth as he talks.

Then another smell hits me. "Is that last week's lunch rotting in there too?"

"Could be." As he starts combing his hair in the mirror, Chuck turns slightly toward Carly.

"There's girls liftin' weights these days too, you know. You could swing by the weight room sometime. I could show you how it's done."

"No thanks," Carly says.

"Your loss." Chuck tosses his comb into his locker, then slams it shut.

As he swaggers off down the hall, Carly turns to me. "I can't believe him. He is the grossest, most obnoxious guy I've ever met. How can he be so totally full of himself?"

I shake my head. "I have no idea, Carly. No idea at all."

Finally it's lunchtime. I'm bolting down the hall when I see Leo.

"Hey, Leo. You've talked to the guys?"

"Yep. Everyone's meeting at my locker after school."

"Right on! Listen, I've got a few things to finish up before then. See you later!"

I rush to the computer lab.

Ms. Kynsi, the computer teacher, looks up from her desk. "Here to do some work, are you, Turk?"

"Yeah." I flop down behind a computer.

For the next half hour, I type frantically. I don't even notice when Ms. Kynsi walks over to my computer.

"Is this a school assignment?"

"Not exactly. My parents—er—cut off my allowance. So I need to find a way to make some money."

"So you're preparing a resume?"

"Not exactly. I'm starting my own business."

"Good for you. What type of business?"

"A—uh—dog-walking business."

"How wonderful! You must really like dogs."

I jump. Is this a trick question? I look closely at Ms. Kynsi and decide it's not.

"Truth is," I lower my voice, "I'm not going to walk the dogs myself."

Ms. Kynsi tips her head to the side. "So then how...?"

"I'm going to be the manager. I'm going to hire some staff to do the work."

"It's great that you have big plans," Ms. Kynsi says. "But most businesspeople start small. They do the work themselves at first. Maybe you should get your dog-walking business up and running before you hire any staff."

She looks like she might laugh when she says the word *staff*.

"I'll keep that in mind," I say coldly. "Can I print this now?"

"Go ahead. The printer's on."

I print ten copies. Then I duck out of the computer lab as fast as I can.

chapter five

"Turk!" Brad spots me first.

"What's this business idea?" Jonathan asks.

"Yeah," Justin says, his face glowing almost as bright as his red hair. "And where are the girls?"

They've got me surrounded at Leo's locker. "Come on outside. I'll explain there."

We stop at a picnic table at the edge of the schoolyard. "Here's how it works. You're all going to become dog walkers."

"Dog walkers?" Kyle sneers. "I'm not spending my spare time with *dogs*. It's *girls* I want."

"I know," I say. "And you know what girls can't resist?"

"I wish I knew." Jonathan scratches his bald head.

"Dogs." I say. "Girls cannot resist dogs. A couple of them made that clear to me this weekend on Whyte Avenue." I smile confidently and wait for my words to sink in.

"For real, Turk? You landed a date?" Brad's eyes are wide behind his glasses.

"Well, not quite. But it was going that way. Just a matter of time."

"Says who?" Kyle asks.

"Says my witness. Tell 'em, Leo."

All eyes turn to Leo, who loves nothing more than an audience.

"Get this," Leo says. "I stepped outside of Starbucks and saw this amazing blond-haired girl. Mal-lor-y–" Leo draws out her name. "She's totally hot. Just like the redhead before her. And guess who she was talking to?" Leo flips his thumb at me.

"She was talking to *Turk*?" Brad says.

"Why would she waste her time with *him*?" Jonathan asks.

"You guys are right," I say. "The girls weren't attracted to me—at least not at first. I had somebody with me who caught their eye: Gretzky."

"You're kidding! What guy *couldn't* land a date if *Gretzky* was with him?" Kyle says.

"Not Gretzky the hockey player," I say. "I'm talking about Gretzky the cockapoo."

"A dog?"

"Yeah, a dog. Or at least a dog to us. To all the girls out there, Gretzky is a total magnet."

Leo nods beside me. "I wouldn't have believed it myself, but Turk is definitely on to something. Girls can't walk by a dog without stopping to pat it and give it a little cuddle."

"And from there," I continue, "guess who they'll want to cuddle next? The guy holding the dog's leash!"

"Are you sure about that?" Kyle says.

"It was working for me," I say.

As the idea sinks in, they all start talking at once.

"So listen," I interrupt them. "Here's the deal. I'll find us some dogs to walk. And I'll collect the money from the owners. Whenever you walk a dog, I'll pay you half the money the owner gives me."

"So when do I get a turn walking Gretzky?" Justin asks.

"Soon. But first I need a few days to set everything up." I hold up the first computer printout. "I'm going to post these ads where people with dogs will see them. Pet food stores, dog grooming salons, vet clinics."

"Good going, Turk," Jonathan says. "There must be hundreds of dogs who need to be walked—hopefully cute, cuddly ones that girls can't resist."

Justin gives a low whistle. "Maybe that will put us up there with the jocks."

"Yeah," Brad says. "The ones who the girls fall all over."

"That's the idea," I say. I hold up the other computer printout. "In the meantime, here is an information sheet. It lists prime meeting spots where you should hang out with the dogs. You know, along Whyte Avenue, by the market on Saturday, at the Hub Mall over at the university and outside coffee shops."

"Wow, Turk. You think of everything," Jonathan says.

I nod. "One last thing. For this to work, we've got to keep a lid on it. If word leaks out, everyone will try the same thing."

"Not good," Kyle says. "I don't plan on sharing my dog-loving girls with anyone."

"Yeah, like with Upchuck and his huge ego," Leo says.

"He's disgusting enough already," Jonathan says. "And that's when he's only in love with himself."

"No kidding," Justin says. "We wouldn't hear the end of it if he stepped into the dating scene."

"Yeah, I can hear it now. Him and his hot dates!"

"Oh gross!" Brad groans. "He'd give the rest of us a bad name."

"Exactly!" I say. "And remember, his locker

is right beside mine. So if you have any questions, catch me in the halls. Or let Leo know. But my locker is off-limits."

"Got it, Turk."

"I'll call another meeting once I've found some dogs for us to walk. Then I'll draw up a schedule and we'll get started. And remember, not a word to anyone."

Everyone leaves, and Leo and I head for home.

"I was just thinking," Leo says. "The dog owners pay you cash up front, right?"

"Right."

"And you keep half of that, right?"

"Right." I smile.

"You should do all right with this, Turk."

"That's the idea. Remember how I can't even pay for a round of hot chocolates?"

"Yeah, tell me about it."

"That's about to change."

Leo thinks some more. "So what about the people who own the dogs? Are you going to tell them why we're walking their dogs? That it's like a dating service?"

"Why would I tell them that? The owners just want their dogs to get some exercise. We'll take good care of their dogs."

"Are you gonna walk some dogs too?"

I shake my head. "Maybe later. For now, I'll just be the brains behind the operation."

Leo nods.

"Actually, Leo." I decide to come clean with him. "Even though I met those two girls Saturday, I didn't know what to say to them. You know, the business *is* a great idea. But I don't think it would work for me."

"Sure it would, Turk. You just need more practice. Like the rest of us."

"I'm not so sure. So for now, I'm gonna let you guys go for it."

"Whatever you say."

That's what I like about Leo. He accepts the answers you give him. He's a hard worker too—rounding up all the guys like that. Maybe I'll give him a bigger cut of the profits, once business takes off.

chapter six

"Turk, get off the phone." Mom fires me a threatening look.

I wave her away. "What was that, Mrs. Nielsen? Weekends only for the next three weeks? Then Wednesdays and Thursdays? Got it. Okay, so I'll pick up Rowdy"—I check my calendar—"nine-thirty Saturday morning."

I turn to Mom. "Okay. I'm done."

"For now." Mom heaves a big sigh. "When

you're not on the family phone these days, you're yakking into your cell phone."

Just then, my cell phone rings. I decide to ignore it.

"I've got a lot of things on, Mom."

"Why does this worry me?"

Dad comes into the kitchen. He's holding two slips of paper. "Here are a couple of phone messages, Turk."

"Thanks, Dad."

Mom gives me a funny look. "You're not up to something, are you?"

"Of course not. At least not what you're probably thinking."

"And what are we probably thinking?"

"That I'm up to something shady."

"Or stupid. Or immoral," Mom adds.

I smile. "I have a new business."

Mom still looks suspicious.

Dad clears his throat. "What kind of business?"

"Dog walking. Like how I walked Gretzky last week. Only with my friends too."

I tell Mom and Dad about the ads I've posted around town and about hiring some guys to help out. For obvious reasons, I leave out the part about meeting girls. When I'm done, they look pretty impressed.

"Sounds like you've hit on a good business venture," Dad says. "Honest money for honest work. Nothing wrong with that."

"I had to do something. Remember that small matter about my allowance getting cut off?" I check their faces for signs of guilt. Nothing.

"Just one question, Turk," Mom says. "Why didn't you tell us sooner?"

Mom must have read another parenting article. I can almost see the headline: *Getting Your Teen to Open Up to You.*

"Well, er...I wanted to get my business running before I said anything. And," I put on my most innocent face, "I had this crazy idea you might think my business was something shady, stupid or immoral."

I can't tell for sure, but I think Mom and Dad almost look ashamed.

Yes!

Dad clears his throat again. "If there's anything we can do to help, let us know."

"Actually, there is something. Do any of your friends have dogs that need to be walked? I could add them to my customer list. Maybe even walk Gretzky again."

Dad nods. "I'll see what I can do."

Dad must have flexed his vice president muscles at work. Along with the people who saw my ads, a bunch of Dad's employees are now on my list. My business has taken off faster than I thought it would. And everyone is happy.

Mom and Dad are happy that I'm working. I'm happy that the cash is rolling in. And my friends are happy that they're connecting with way more girls than usual.

"Turk, I got a phone number from this girl I met at the market on Saturday," Justin says. "She loves Axel the black lab. We're seeing a movie together on the weekend."

"Man! You gotta send me out with Pepper again," Kyle says. "Lisa from the Hub Mall says he's *just adorable*."

"Please tell me that Bogart needs a walk this weekend," Jonathan begs. "I've gotta cross paths again with Jessica. She *loved* Bogart!"

Even though the guys are totally enthused about the business, I'm learning quickly that there are some dogs they just don't want to walk. Especially Rowdy.

Rowdy belongs to Mrs. Nielsen, a lady who does shift work. According to Mrs. Nielsen, her two-year-old yellow lab was rowdy when she first got him, and he still is. Man, she's not kidding about that!

All of the guys complained that he scared away the girls. He's just too rowdy. He jumps up on anyone who comes near. So guess who ends up walking Rowdy? Me. Definitely not what I had in mind.

The bigger surprise though—thanks to Rowdy—is that my own love life takes a turn for the better.

It starts the first time I take Rowdy for a walk. It's Saturday afternoon and Rowdy is bouncing from one side of me to the other.

"Sorry about that," I say to an alarmed-looking woman. Rowdy has just lunged hard toward her. For about the tenth time, he's almost pulled my arms out of their sockets.

"He's really friendly," I say as she steps away from us. "Too friendly, really." I can tell she doesn't believe me.

Right now, Rowdy and I are cruising across the university campus toward the physed building. We're almost at that big yellow gym called the Butterdome when a voice calls from behind me.

"Turk?"

I look up and nearly trip over Rowdy.

"Carly?"

As usual, Carly looks like she's been running. Her hair is in a ponytail, and she's breathing a bit hard. As she gets closer, I read her T-shirt. It says something about a race in Banff. Even with a sweaty T-shirt and a red face, Carly looks terrific.

Why haven't I noticed that before?

Rowdy interrupts my thoughts by pulling hard on his leash. I hang on as Rowdy tries to lunge toward the dog that Carly is holding beside her.

"Sorry about that," I say.

"It's okay," Carly says. "Buddy usually likes other dogs."

"Buddy?"

"Yeah." Carly smiles down at her dog and pats his head. "Buddy isn't the most original name for a dog. But it made sense when I got him."

"Oh. Uh, why's that?"

"I got Buddy just after Dad moved away four years ago. Mom was a wreck. My brother, Matt, was too wrapped up in his girlfriend and his football team to notice. So I got Buddy. I needed one right then. A buddy, I mean."

I should say something. But as usual, my voice doesn't work well in front of a good-looking girl. And it's hitting me good and hard that that's exactly what Carly is.

"Er, what kind of dog is Buddy?" I finally choke out.

"I'm not sure. I got Buddy from the Humane Society. He was abandoned when he was a puppy. The Humane Society people think he's part German shepherd and part lab. Maybe part husky too."

Carly shrugs her shoulders, then turns to Rowdy. "Who's this?"

"Rowdy. Guess how he got *his* name?"

Carly laughs as Rowdy tries to start a wrestling match with Buddy.

"Rowdy belongs to a lady in our neighborhood. She works these crazy shifts and can't always walk him. Rowdy has tons of energy, so she hired me to walk him."

I can't resist trying to impress Carly. "Rowdy's part of my dog-walking business. I've hired my friends to walk most of the dogs. But I walk Rowdy myself."

Rowdy bounces even higher when he hears his name.

"A dog-walking business. Cool." Carly smiles and I nearly melt.

Think of something to say, Turk!

"We'd better keep going," Carly says. "Buddy and I just finished a run and we're on our way home. See you Monday."

She takes off down the sidewalk with Buddy beside her.

"Yeah, see you," I mutter.

That's when it hits me. I should have offered to walk her and Buddy home! Next time, I'll be ready!

chapter seven

As it turns out, I don't have to wait until Monday to talk to Carly again.

"It's for you—as usual," Mom says, handing me the phone the next morning.

"Hello?"

"Hi, Turk. It's Carly."

A hot red blush covers my face. I turn away so Mom won't notice.

"Turk, I got this idea after I saw you."

Yeah, I got a few ideas myself!

"Er...what idea is that?" I ask.

"I've been training for a race. It's Saturday morning in Calgary. Mom and I are leaving Friday at noon and we need someone to walk Buddy Friday night."

"What about your brother?"

I could kick myself the minute the words spill out of my big stupid mouth.

"Matt says he's too busy studying for an exam. Can you walk Buddy Friday night? Mom will pay you."

Of course I'd agree to *anything* Carly wants.

"Sure thing, Carly." I write down her address. "Will your brother be home then?"

"Yeah. He'll have Buddy ready for you."

"Okay." I scribble into my calendar. "I've scheduled Buddy in for Friday night at seven o'clock."

"Thanks, Turk. And one more thing. You said that your friends walk most of your customers' dogs, right?"

"Right. Leo and Kyle and some of the guys."

Carly's quiet for a moment. "I need to ask a favor. Those guys—I know they're all right.

But could you please walk Buddy yourself? So I know he's in good hands. Can you do that for me?"

Anything!

"No problem. Buddy and me—we'll have fun walking together Friday night. I'll take good care of him."

"I know you will, Turk. Thanks again."

I hang up the phone and pump my fist into the air. "Yes!"

"What's that all about?"

I jump. I forgot that Mom was still here.

"Oh nothing. Just business, you know. Another happy customer."

I smile, and then bounce out of the kitchen.

I catch up with Leo and the guys at lunchtime on Monday.

"Did you schedule me in for prime time this week, Turk? Friday night? Saturday night maybe?" Justin asks.

"Yeah, what about me? Any calls about the basset hound?" Brad pushes his glasses back up on his nose. "The girls were all over Basil last week."

"Hey, I get the basset hound this time," Kyle elbows him. "I already told Turk I wanted him."

"Basil's no better than Cyril. You know— the great Dane?" Jonathan says. "Girls from far and wide wanted to pat Cyril last weekend."

"I could do without Tex this week," Kyle says. "Unless his owner has given him a bath. Tex doesn't have much appeal."

"Yeah, nobody came close to Tex last week either," Justin says. "What's the point?"

"What do you mean, 'what's the point'?" I glare at Justin.

Justin's face turns redder than his hair. "You know," he says. "Tex doesn't stir up interest. It's not his fault or anything."

Kyle jumps in. "He just doesn't pull in the girls like the cuter dogs do."

"Yeah. Remember why we're doing this, Turk," Jonathan says.

"Maybe you should remind me."

"Hello! To meet girls!" Justin says.

"Yeah, Turk. What are you getting so uptight about?"

I don't answer. Instead, I shove a schedule into everyone's hand.

"What's with him?" Kyle mutters.

I don't really know myself. All I know is that Carly's words about Buddy keep running through my head. How Buddy helped see her through a bad time and how special he is. Maybe the other dog owners feel that way about their dogs too. The dogs we've just spent part of our lunch rating for how well they attract girls.

I don't say anything for the rest of the lunch period. When the bell rings, everyone stands up to leave. Except me.

Leo's partway out the cafeteria door when he sees that I'm still sitting at the table.

"You coming, Turk?"

"Yeah. I guess." It feels like I weigh a ton as I pull myself up from the table. I follow my friends down the hall.

chapter eight

I'm at my locker on Wednesday when the week takes a turn for the better.

"Have you been walking Rowdy much lately?" Carly asks.

"Yeah, a bit. I'm walking him tomorrow night again."

Then I remember what I wished I'd said on Saturday.

"Carly?"

"Yeah?"

I swallow hard. "I'm picking Rowdy up

at seven o'clock tomorrow night. If you and Buddy were maybe going for a walk, Rowdy and I could swing by your place first. We could grab a Coke or something."

Carly gives me this sweet smile, straight into my face, and I almost keel over. "That'd be great, Turk. I train at the university after school. But I'll still have time to shower and eat dinner before you come over."

Then Carly stops, red-faced, as though she just realized she's been babbling. The truth is I could listen to her babble all day.

Suddenly I realize that someone else is listening too.

"A date. How sweet."

I glance over my shoulder at Chuck. He has a bodybuilding magazine propped open in his locker. He's admiring himself in the mirror as he copies the poses in the magazine. Chuck turns to Carly. "So you said yes to the Turk Man?"

"We're walking our dogs together. Okay?"

"How sweet. Walking your puppies together. Puppy love..."

"Listen, you jerk. I happen to have a dog-walking business. It's my job, okay?" I glance sideways at Carly. I love the way she's looking at me while I'm laying into Chuck. "So don't sweat it that Carly and I are—"

Then I stop. I've said enough. Or maybe too much. I shut up before I say anything else about the business.

Time to change the subject—*fast!*

"Don't you have laundry to do, Chuck? Or maybe some food to stuff into your face?"

"Oh yeah! Time for some more protein!" Chuck pulls out a half-empty box of energy bars from under a pile of dirty sweat socks.

"Yuck!" Carly cringes as we take off for first class.

Then I start wishing that I hadn't mentioned my business to Chuck. But with Carly walking beside me down the hall, I have better things to think about. There's no harm done anyway. Chuck was probably so busy flexing in front of his mirror that he's forgotten about my dog-walking business already.

So then my thoughts start going more like this: *Right on, Turk! You actually asked her. And, she said yes!*

After school I check in with the guys at Leo's locker.

"Everyone's still okay with the schedule for the week?"

"No, there's a problem. Justin went home sick this morning," Leo says. "Isn't he supposed to walk Axel tonight?"

"Yeah. At seven-thirty. Who can cover him?"

"I can take Axel, but not until eight o'clock."

"Sounds good," I say. "I'll phone Axel's owner and change his time to eight o'clock."

I check the schedule once more. "Justin's on for Friday night too. He'll probably be better by then. If not, who's free?"

No one speaks up.

"You might be on, boss," Kyle says.

I remember that I'm walking Buddy on Friday night. As if I'd forget that!

"I can't."

"Why not?" Brad asks.

"I'm walking another dog Friday night."

"Is it Rowdy?" Leo asks.

"No. I only walk Rowdy on Thursday and Sunday this week."

"Quit holding out, Turk. Who's the dog?" Kyle asks.

"Probably some knockout girl-magnet dog that Turk's been keeping to himself," Jonathan laughs.

"Yeah, like a golden retriever puppy," Brad says.

"Or a cute little dalmatian that the girls will fall all over."

"You're all wrong," I say. "It's a German shepherd, crossed with black lab, crossed with husky. We think."

"Oh." They look at me blankly.

Kyle speaks up first. "Doesn't sound like a top-scorer. Why are you walking *that* dog?"

I glare at him before I answer. "He belongs to Carly."

No one says anything at first. But then it starts.

"I get it now," Leo says.

"I thought you had your eye on her," Jonathan says.

"Good going, Turk!"

"So it's Carly, eh?" Kyle elbows me.

"Hey," Leo interrupts, "I've got some other news you're all gonna want to hear. We're invited to a party Saturday night."

"Whose party?" Jonathan asks.

"Meghan's." Leo smiles broadly.

"Did you say Meghan? As in your beautiful popular cousin?"

"That's the one. My aunt and uncle are throwing Meghan a huge party for her birthday. They told me to invite my friends."

Talk about excitement! The comments fly as the guys jostle each other down the hallway.

As Leo closes his locker, he says, "What's up, Turk? Aren't you excited about the party?"

"I guess. But this business is getting to me. It's not as much fun as it used to be."

"Hmm. It must be tough being the boss.

Everyone fighting over the same dogs—the ones that draw the most girls."

"It's not just that," I say. "It's how they talk about some of the dogs—like they're total rejects."

"You mean like we used to be? Before we started meeting girls and getting invited to parties—like on Saturday night?"

I can tell Leo is really pumped about Meghan's party. He couldn't wait to swing the conversation back around to it. And really, it's not like we get invited to parties every day.

"You're right, Leo. It'll be great!"

Leo nods. "Yeah. Why don't you invite Carly?"

A big grin takes over my face. "You know, Leo? I just might do that!"

Things are definitely looking up.

chapter nine

Thursday night takes forever to roll around. But finally, I'm heading out the front door to meet Carly for our walk.

Mom glances over. "You look nice."

"Thanks."

She looks at me suspiciously. "Aren't you walking Rowdy tonight?"

"Yeah. I'm on my way to pick him up now." Then I add, "I'm picking up a friend, too. She has a dog. We're going to walk the dogs together."

"Ohhh," Mom says. "Kind of like...a date?"

I can see the headline from Mom's parenting magazine: *Communicating with Your Teen About Dating*.

"Does this friend have a name?"

"Yeah, she does." I close the door behind me.

Even through the closed door, I can hear Mom's voice. "Turk! Turk!"

I laugh as I race down the driveway.

By the time I've picked up Rowdy and walked to Carly's house, Carly is waiting outside with Buddy.

"Hey, Carly."

"Hi, Turk. How's it going, Rowdy?"

At the sound of his name, Rowdy lunges even harder toward them. Then Buddy dodges between Carly and Rowdy.

"I think someone's jealous," Carly says, nodding at Buddy.

Carly and I laugh as we untangle Buddy's and Rowdy's leashes.

"We'd better get these guys moving," Carly says. "Which way?"

"To the Hub Mall?"

"Sure."

As we head to the university, Buddy and Rowdy pull hard on their leashes. It's like they've both decided that they have to be the leader.

"Does Buddy usually pull you like this?"

"Not usually," Carly says. "What about Rowdy?"

"Always."

Carly laughs.

"It looks like Buddy's gone this way before," I say.

"Hundreds of times. Mom works at the physed building. Any minute now, Buddy's going to veer toward the Butterdome."

Sure enough, two seconds later, Buddy tries to pull Carly toward the Butterdome.

"Where should I take Buddy for our walk tomorrow night?"

"He likes it around here and by the Kinsmen Sports Center down the hill. He gets excited watching the runners take off from outside the gym."

We walk in silence for a few minutes and are soon at the Hub Mall.

"If you want to run in for drinks," Carly says, "I'll hold Buddy and Rowdy."

"Deal," I say. "What do you want to drink?"

"Umm, surprise me."

"Might be risky. What if I get you something you can't stand?"

"I'll take my chances."

I hand Rowdy's leash to Carly. "I'll be back in a few minutes."

I can't resist a backward glance at Carly and the dogs as I open the door to the Hub Mall. Carly is laughing as Buddy pushes Rowdy away to stand closer to Carly.

I'm with you there, Buddy!

I scope out the vendors inside the mall. A yogurt smoothie? I don't think so. A Coke? Nah. Then I see it.

"Can I have two chocolate milkshakes?"

"Here you are," I tell Carly minutes later.

Carly looks into the see-through lid. "Chocolate milkshake?"

"The finest," I say.

"Umm-hmmm," Carly says, taking a long drink from the straw.

I take Rowdy's leash from Carly, and we walk across the campus.

"Do you think you might end up here some day?" Carly asks me.

"Where?"

"Here. Studying at the university."

"I haven't thought about it," I say. "I pretty much take things one day at a time."

Carly laughs. "So you're *almost* thinking about tomorrow then?"

"Yeah. When Buddy and I do our solo walk. Right, Buddy?"

When he hears his name, Buddy trots back and licks my hand. Then he bounds in front of us, trying to get ahead of Rowdy again.

"He likes you," Carly says. "I'm so glad. I don't like leaving Buddy with just anyone. He's too special."

"I meant what I said before, Carly. I'll take good care of Buddy tomorrow night. We'll have a great time. Just us guys! And I'll get him back home safely."

"Thanks, Turk." Then Carly does something that I don't expect. She stops. She turns. And she kisses me. Square on the mouth. Then she starts walking again. As though nothing out of the ordinary just happened.

I smile to myself as we circle back toward her house.

Good going! I haven't blown it yet tonight! So while I'm on a roll—

"Carly, there's this birthday party Saturday night. At Meghan's house. I don't know when you're back from Calgary. Or maybe you're too tired to go out after you've run a race...," *I'm starting to lose it.* "...But if you think you might like to go to the party—"

"I'd love to go the party with you, Turk."

"Really?"

We're at Carly's driveway now. I don't want Carly to go in, but I'm almost relieved that the night is ending before I blow it somehow.

"Yeah, really," Carly says. "And by the way, I'm only at school tomorrow for the morning. Mom and I are leaving for Calgary at lunchtime. To avoid the traffic."

"So I might not see you tomorrow?"

"Maybe not. Maybe not until Saturday night."

"At seven o'clock."

"See you Saturday night then," Carly says softly.

"Yeah."

And as Carly bounds into her house, I mutter to myself, "I can't wait!"

chapter ten

At school on Friday, I see Carly for only a second.

"Hey, Turk!" Carly calls over her shoulder as she bounds down the hall. "See you tomorrow!"

"Looks like your business is working."

I jump and turn around.

"You're doing okay with the girls, right Stick Man?" Chuck drawls. "Or at least with *one* of them."

Oh no! Does Chuck know more about the business than I think?

"What are you talking about?"

"I'm talking about Carly, you doofus. You know—Runner Girl?" I'm so tense that I barely catch the whiff of underarm sweat as Chuck reaches up to comb his hair.

"I don't mean about Carly. I mean about my dog-walking business. You said—"

"That you've hit on a real brainwave. I've gotta hand it to you, man. The girls are all over the dogs. Then the girls are all over the guy who's holding the dog's leash."

I freeze on the spot. Except for my stomach, which does a huge back-flip.

"Now add this to the picture," Chuck says, "a guy who is big and"—he tosses his comb aside and strikes a pose—"*built*! It's brilliant!"

He knows!

"So Turk, maybe you could deal me in on the action. Come to think of it, I don't have anything on tonight."

I slam my locker shut and take off to class. I need to clear my head—decide my next move—before I can deal with Chuck. First I'm going to find out who blabbed. Then...well, then I don't know *what* I'm going to do.

At Leo's locker after school, I ask them, "Who told Chuck about the business?"

"What do you mean?" Leo says. "No one would tell *Chuck*."

"Wrong. Someone did. Chuck knows everything about the business. Everything." I wait while my words sink in. "Who was it?"

No one says anything. I look at all of them in turn. They all meet my eyes. Except Kyle.

"Kyle?"

"Chuck already knew about the business before I said a word," Kyle protests. "He said you told him all about it."

I shake my head. "All I'd told him was that we walk dogs. Not that we walk dogs to meet girls! He didn't know that part!" I realize I'm yelling.

And now Kyle is yelling too. "I'm supposed to know what you told him and what you didn't tell him? Chuck was yakking on about your dog-walking business—that *you* told *him* about. And *I'm* supposed to know you didn't tell him about meeting girls?"

Kyle pauses long enough to catch his breath. But only so he can yell at me some more. "So you wanna know who blabbed? I'll tell you, Turk. *You* did!"

In the silence that follows, I realize that Kyle's right. If I hadn't been showing off in front of Carly, Chuck wouldn't know anything about the business at all.

I don't know what to say. I clear my throat and pull out the schedule I gave the guys last Monday.

"So the schedule's still okay for everyone?"

"Except Justin's still sick," Jonathan says.

"Still?"

"Yeah, puking like crazy." Everyone groans.

"So who can walk Axel tonight?"

Silence.

"I'm meeting Rachel for a movie," Jonathan says.

"What about you, Brad? Can you walk Axel and Gretzky tonight? They'd be okay together."

"No, Turk. I was just about to tell you. I can't walk any dogs tonight. We have to drive to Camrose. My grandmother fell and broke her wrist. We've gotta go help her out."

"Tonight?"

"Yep."

"Is anyone else free tonight?"

No answer. I'm getting desperate.

"Leo, can you help? Around seven?"

"Well, maybe. But I'll be a bit late. I've gotta walk all the way to Parkallen to pick up Pepper."

"That's okay. We can make this work. I'll get Buddy and bring him back to my house. Then I'll pick up Axel and Gretzky. Axel will be at my place for you to pick up just after seven. Then I'll walk Buddy and Gretzky."

"That should work," Leo says.

"Thanks, Leo."

"No problem."

"Yeah. No problem."

chapter eleven

Mom's in the kitchen when I whip in for some food.

"Turk, I was thinking. We haven't had much quality family time lately. Maybe tonight we could—"

"Not tonight, Mom. I've got a whole ton of dogs to walk. Justin's sick. Brad's out of town."

"Sounds serious."

"Yeah." I down some milk, then throw together a cheese sandwich.

"You know," Mom says, "maybe Dad and I could help. We're really proud of how responsibly you've been running your business. Your father has been hearing good things from the people he works with too. In fact," Mom's eyes widen, "if you want to bring the dogs here, Dad and I can help you walk them."

It's hardly my idea of a good time. But it just might help with all the dogs Leo and I need to walk tonight. Not to mention getting another round of quality family time out of the way.

"Sure, Mom. Thanks."

"I'll put together some dinner for Dad and me. Then we'll get ready for some dog walking."

Dad gets home a few minutes later. At first he's surprised when Mom tells him the plan for the evening. But he bounces back fast when she leans heavily into the words quality family time.

Minutes later, I'm heading out the door.

"I have to get Buddy. I'll be back in a few minutes."

Ten minutes later, I'm introducing Buddy to Mom and Dad.

Mom looks at Buddy. Then she eyes her Persian rug.

"It's okay, Mom. Buddy's house-trained."

"Yes, of course." But she still looks worried.

"I've gotta pick up Axel and Gretzky now. I won't be long. Have fun with Buddy!"

"Sure, Turk," Dad says as I crash out the front door again.

"Okay. Now I've got everyone," I pant as I stumble back inside with Axel and Gretzky fifteen minutes later.

"Did Leo come by yet?"

"He did," Mom said. "He was going to wait here until you got back with Axel. But I told him to go have a nice walk with that little dog he'd already picked up."

"But we had it all planned. He was going to walk Axel too. I don't like changing the plan at the last minute like this. In case something goes wrong."

"What could go wrong?"

I shrug. "Nothing, I guess. You and Dad and me can still manage three dogs."

"You mean *two* dogs," Dad says.

"Two?"

That doesn't make sense. I look around the corner into the living room.

"Where's Buddy?" My voice comes out in a whisper.

"Buddy's already started his walk," Mom says. "Just before Leo arrived, another one of your friends came by to walk one of the dogs. We sent him away with Buddy."

"Oh no! Carly asked me to walk Buddy myself."

"Turk, settle down," Dad says. "I'm sure you've only hired trustworthy young men for your business. Buddy will be fine with someone else tonight."

He's probably right. But still, I promised Carly.

"The guys all said they were busy tonight," I say. "So who picked up Buddy?"

"It was somebody I haven't met before," Mom says. "What was his name again, Mack?"

"Chuck, wasn't it?"

"That's it. Chuck!" Mom says.

"*Not Chuck!*"

"Turk, settle down. Chuck seemed perfectly polite and respectable—"

"That's what you think!"

"And he said he'd be back with Buddy in an hour."

I grab Axel and Gretzky's leashes and clip them onto the dogs. Then I face Mom and Dad. "You two stay here. We're going looking for Chuck and Buddy. If they come back while I'm out, call me on my cell."

We shoot out the door. Axel and Gretzky are surprised that we're running down the sidewalk instead of doing our usual walk. Axel soon gets into it, but I have to scoop Gretzky up and carry her under my arm like a football.

Where would they have gone?

Think like Chuck, I tell myself.

But that's no help. From what I can tell, Chuck isn't what you'd call a deep thinker.

Okay, then think like Buddy.

The university!

With Gretzky still under my arm, Axel and I bolt over to the campus. I veer toward the Butterdome like Buddy did earlier this week.

"Buddy! Bud-dy!" I call.

As I run, I think about how badly I want to beat the crap out of Chuck. And if anything happens to Buddy, I swear...

We're almost at the Butterdome.

"Buddy!"

No answer. No sign of Chuck and Buddy at all.

I've circled almost all the way around the Butterdome when my cell phone rings.

"Yeah?"

"Turk, it's your mother."

"I know it's you. Where's Buddy?"

"He's here. And he's perfectly fine. Just like I told you he would be."

"You're sure?"

"Of course I'm sure. You should feel very foolish. All that fuss for nothing," Mom says.

"Did Chuck say anything when he brought Buddy back?"

"Just to let you know that he *scored big* with Buddy tonight. Whatever that means."

Let's not go there, Mom!

I try to catch my breath. "So Buddy's there with you? Right now?"

"Of course."

"Don't let him out of your sight. I'll be home soon."

I run all the way home. Buddy runs to greet me when I burst through the door.

"Hey, Buddy. Sorry about tonight, boy. You're okay?" I rub his ear.

"For heaven's sake, Turk. He's fine. You've made a big deal out of nothing."

"No comment," I say. "I'm going to take the dogs home now."

"Do you want your mother and me to help?"

I don't answer. I just slam the door shut behind me.

First I drop Gretzky off. Then Axel. I keep Buddy with me until last. It's like I'm still trying to keep my promise to Carly about walking Buddy—even though I've already screwed up big time.

Matt opens the door when I ring the doorbell. Jeez, he fills up the whole doorway. What did Carly say Matt does? Football? Wrestling? Something like that. He's huge!

"Hi, uh, Matt. Here's Buddy." I hand him Buddy's leash. "We...er...had a good walk tonight."

I turn to go.

"Wait. Mom left you a check. For walking Buddy."

"Thanks."

I'm partway down the driveway when Matt calls me back.

"Hey," he says.

"Yeah?"

"Are you a runner?"

"Uh, no. Why?"

"Looks like you've been running."

I'd rather not have to explain why I was running like crazy tonight.

"No way," I say. "I'm actually allergic to my own sweat."

Matt looks at me like I've just stepped off another planet.

As I step onto the sidewalk, I realize that what I've been blinking away for a while now is sweat. So that's why Matt looked at me so funny.

Then as I'm shivering in my sweaty T-shirt, I realize what's happened. It's not just the running that had me sweating tonight. I was worried about Buddy. Not just because he's Carly's dog. But because he's a good guy, and I wouldn't want anything to happen to him. Or to any of the other dogs.

That's it! It's the *dogs*. Wouldn't you know it! The *dogs* have gotten to me!

chapter twelve

When Leo phones me on my cell the next day, he says, "You sound half dead. What's up?"

"I ran around the university last night."

"You gotta be kidding! Not the guy who tries to dodge every gym class he possibly can! Not the guy who's—"

"I know. Allergic to his own sweat."

"Yeah. So what's with the running then?"

I pour out the whole story.

Leo gives a low whistle. "So what're you gonna do now? You gonna tell Carly that Upchuck walked her dog last night?"

"I don't know yet."

"*Turk!*"

"Hang on, Leo. Mom's calling me."

"Mom, I'm on my cell." I step out onto the staircase.

She holds the cordless phone toward me.

"It's for you. It's Carly."

Carly? What am I going to say to her!

"Listen, Leo—"

"Yeah, I heard. It's Carly. Catch you later."

"Hey, Carly." I shift phones as I walk back into my bedroom.

"Turk, how's it going?"

"Good. Er...so you're home, eh?"

"Yeah. Mom and I just got in an hour ago."

"How was your race?"

"Awesome! I finished second in my age group. The winner beat me by just a few seconds. I had her almost until the end."

"Right on, Carly. You'll beat her next time."

"I hope so," Carly says. "But still, that's the fastest I've ever run a five-mile race."

"You ran five miles today, rode back from Calgary, and you're still alive?"

"Yeah," Carly laughs. "And, I'm going out partying with you in a few hours. Remember?"

"No way I'd forget *that*."

"Me either. It'll be fun. I was thinking about the party when I was running this morning."

"Maybe that's why you didn't win. Aren't you supposed to think about running faster than everyone else?"

"Yeah, maybe," Carly laughs. "But there's something else I phoned about. To thank you for walking Buddy last night."

Suddenly that warm glow I'd been feeling vanishes.

I've gotta tell her!

But Carly continues. "Matt said that you and Buddy were gone longer than an hour. When Mom heard that, she asked me to check if we should pay you more."

I glance over at the check lying on my dresser.

Tell her what happened, Turk.

"Uh, you know, Carly. I've got the check here. But your mom—she doesn't have to pay me at all—"

"Mom insists on paying you, Turk. And I liked knowing that Buddy was with you last night."

I cringe when Carly says that last part. If there's a time to tell Carly the truth—before it's too late—it's *now*.

"So you'll come by around seven o'clock?"

"Yeah."

"Good. See you then."

All the way to Carly's place, I practice what I'm going to say about last night. That it was a mix-up. That I'm sorry. And that I didn't tell her earlier because I wanted to say it in person.

Then Carly comes to the door. She's wearing her hair down long tonight. It looks all shiny and soft, like she just brushed it.

I'm thinking about maybe kissing her, but I'm not sure. I wonder if Carly's thinking about the same thing.

"Ahem."

We both jump.

"Oh. Mom." Carly giggles as a deep blush spreads across her cheeks.

"Are you going to introduce me to your friend?"

"Yeah." Carly giggles again. "This is Turk. Turk, this is my mom."

"Hi, Mrs.–er..."

"Ms. Lawton. Katie, actually." She reaches out to shake my hand. Carly's mom looks a lot like Carly. She's taller but has Carly's brown hair and big dark eyes.

"So you're off to a party tonight."

"Y-yeah," I stammer. "It's not far. Lots of kids from school will be there."

"Sounds like fun. You two enjoy."

You can count on that!

We head out the door and I take Carly's hand. I'm flying. And we're not even at the party yet.

It looks like about half the school is already at Meghan's place when Carly and I get there.

"Carly!" Lexia squeals as she opens the front door. "Come on in! This party is *such* a blast!"

Lexia grabs our arms and hauls us into the room.

"Look who's here, everyone!" she yells over the music. "It's Carly and—and—"

"Turk," I say.

"Yeah, Turk!" Lexia shrieks. "You two *have* to come up and dance."

Lexia wiggles out a few dance moves to lure us onto the dance floor. I swallow hard. I sure hope Carly doesn't expect me to *dance* tonight. Definitely not my thing!

I look around desperately. Meghan's mom is carrying trays of fruit and cheese over to a long food table that's already piled high with cold cuts and buns and cookies and chips. That's more my style! I glance at Carly.

Carly smiles then turns to Lexia. "Maybe we'll just grab some food first."

Yes! Saved!

"Sure thing," Lexia says, looking disappointed. "But *later*"—she pulls off a few more moves—"later for *sure!*"

As we make our way over to the table, I lean in to Carly. "That was close!"

"You're not kidding!" Carly laughs.

Just then, Leo waves from the far end of the table.

"Go ahead, Turk," Carly says when she sees Leo. "I'm going to go say hi to my friends."

Carly makes her way through the crowd toward the living room.

"Hey, Turk," Leo says. He's standing in front of an enormous punch bowl. "Aunt Gail asked me to pour drinks. I figure it's a prime spot for meeting some girls tonight." Then he bows as though he's a waiter. "Would you like some punch, sir?"

"Sure."

Leo shoves a cup of punch at me and nods in Carly's direction. "Everything okay with Carly? You know—about last night?"

Just then, Carly looks over and smiles. I smile back. Then I decide something: I'm going to just enjoy myself tonight.

"Awesome. And speaking of Carly, I'm going to stop wasting my time here with you."

"Yeah, go for it. And Turk?"

"Yeah?"

"Cheers!" Leo bashes his glass of punch against mine. Punch sloshes over the rim and down my arm. I shake off as much as I can. "Later, Leo."

I head toward the living room to meet Carly. But more people are arriving all the time. Now the room is totally packed. There's a big traffic jam near the door where Lexia is still trying to haul people onto the dance floor. Then there's the huge mob of girls who have swarmed Meghan to check out her birthday gifts. So it's a while before I can get to Carly.

"Hey," I say, "why don't we go downstairs. Maybe it's not so crowded in the basement."

"Sure."

On our way through, I see Jonathan and Justin by the food table. Both are digging into the chips and salsa and are happily flicking salsa at each other. But then I spot someone else. The last guy I want to see tonight: *Chuck*.

"Uh, Carly. Let's go back to the dining room. I'll get you some punch."

"No thanks. I don't want any punch right now."

"W-well, I wouldn't mind some."

"Okay." Carly shrugs and turns around.

"*Turk!*" Somehow Chuck manages to bellow over top of all the noise in the room.

I keep walking, pushing Carly along in front of me.

At that moment the music stops. Lexia dashes to the stereo and starts fumbling through some CD's. But it's gotten really quiet.

"Turk!" A huge hand claps down on my shoulder from behind.

"Hey, Chuck." I try to shrug his hand off, but he doesn't move it. Carly has stopped in front of me. I'm trapped.

"Uh, Chuck. I thought you'd be lifting weights tonight. Or maybe plastering some gel into your hair." I'm trying really hard to shut Chuck up before he says anything about walking Buddy last night.

"Nah. All taken care of, Stick Man." I try to duck the spray of spit that I know is coming. Unfortunately I don't totally manage it.

"Great," I say. "Enjoy the party."

I'm turning away when Chuck grabs my shoulder again.

"Listen, man. We've got some business to sort out," he shouts.

"I doubt it, Chuck," I say. "Listen, the food's over there. Don't you need to go and beef up? You look a bit thin tonight."

I wonder why no one has started the music up again.

"Really?" Chuck examines his right bicep closely. "But, Turk, *listen*—"

"I'm sure everyone is listening, Chuck." I say this quietly, hoping Chuck will take the hint and lower his voice.

"You gotta pay me. You know—for walking Buddy last night," he yells. "As for that business of yours, it works! You've nailed it, man! Girls *love* dogs! Even dogs like Buddy that aren't exactly pretty! You shoulda seen the girls checkin' out Buddy and me when we were walking along Whyte Avenue."

Won't this guy ever shut up?

"Your folks said you weren't home to pay me last night. So cough up the dough."

I'm still holding Carly's hand. I haven't looked at her since Chuck started blatting his big stupid head off. Now I glance sideways at her.

Carly's eyes are wide, and her mouth—that mouth that I wanted to kiss again tonight—is open in shock.

Carly pulls her hand away. "You let *Chuck* walk *Buddy* last night?"

"Carly, here's what happened—"

"I just heard what happened! This creep walked Buddy. After you promised you'd walk him yourself."

"It wasn't like that."

"But isn't it true? Did Chuck walk Buddy last night?"

"Well, yeah. But—"

Carly pushes through the mob of people and rushes outside. She's almost at the road before I catch up with her. "Carly. *Wait!*" I reach for her hand.

"Don't touch me. Why don't you just go back in and party with your friend, Chuck? Maybe talk some more *business* with him?"

"Can you just listen for a minute?" I reach into my back pocket. "Here. It's your mom's check. Can you give it back to her for me? I don't feel right keeping it."

Carly shoves my arm away. If she wasn't mad before, she sure is now.

"What? You think it's just about the money? You're an even bigger jerk than I thought."

Then Carly turns and runs down the road. I see for myself why she almost won that race in Calgary today. There's no way I can catch up with her.

"Carly! *Carly!*"

"I think you've seen the last of her for tonight," Leo says from behind me. "Sorry."

chapter thirteen

Mom is shaking my shoulders the next morning. "Turk, you need to get up!"

"Why?"

"You have to go see that woman who does shift work. She's been phoning and phoning. You're late taking Rowdy for his walk."

"Oh. I slept in." The truth is, I didn't fall asleep until really late last night.

I pull on my clothes and am about to rush over to Mrs. Nielsen's house. But there's something I need to do first. I grab my cell phone and dial Carly's number.

"Hello?"

Oh no! It's Matt!

"Hello. Er...is Carly there?"

"Yeah. Just a second."

"Carly!" Matt is holding the phone near his mouth. I can hear everything perfectly.

"Who is it?" Carly asks.

"How am I supposed to know?"

"You could ask," Carly says.

"Uh, who is it?" Matt asks.

"Turk."

"It's Turk," Matt tells Carly.

"Tell him he's the last person in this world I plan on talking to!" Moments later I hear a door slam. It hits me like a hard slap in the face.

Matt comes back on the phone. "She can't come to the phone right now."

I don't know for sure, but I picture a big sneer across Matt's face.

"That's okay," I mutter.

But really, it's *not* okay. It's not okay at all.

"Sorry I'm late," I say when I get to Mrs. Nielsen's house.

"No problem. But that was a long shift." She yawns. "I need to get to bed."

"Sure thing," I sigh.

"Actually, Turk, you look as tired as I do. Are you sick or something?"

"Yeah. Or something." But I don't think she hears me. Rowdy has obviously figured out that we're going for a walk. He's barking and bouncing like crazy. It takes both Mrs. Nielsen and me to get his leash on.

We head outdoors and Rowdy pulls me across the road. Then he lunges hard toward some trails we've taken before. Today, I don't even try to resist. I just let Rowdy drag me wherever he wants. And once we get going, there doesn't seem like much point in stopping.

I eventually realize that we've walked pretty far. We're on a trail in the river valley just past the Kinsmen Sports Center. As I watch all the runners take off, I feel even worse. They remind me of Carly.

I stop on a bench. By now, even Rowdy is happy to rest. I reach over and rub his ear.

"What would *you* do, Rowdy, if you screwed up big time like I just did?" It takes me a second to choke the next words out. "And Rowdy, I really like her. *Really*. What am I gonna do?"

I hear a shuffle in the bushes behind me. I jump and look over my shoulder. It's another dog. This dog is mostly black with white hairs around his mouth. He must be old. When he hears my voice, he trudges over to the bench beside me. I look around for the dog's owner, but the dog is by himself.

"Hey, guy. What are you doing here all alone?"

Rowdy sniffs the old dog, then flops back down on the other side of me. I pat both dogs from the bench. "Want to hang out with us for a while?"

Rowdy and this new dog both look at me with big kind eyes. Buddy has eyes like that too. I remember what Carly told me about Buddy seeing her through the tough times when her dad moved away. I didn't really get it then. But with the two dogs lying peacefully beside me, I'm getting the picture.

I hear another shuffle down the path and a woman rushes toward us. She runs over and hugs the dog.

Then she turns to me. "Mickey usually waits on the front step when I go inside for his water dish. I don't know why he took off today. Thanks for looking after him."

"I didn't really do anything. He just joined Rowdy and me here."

"He can tell who the dog lovers are." The whole time, Rowdy has been leaning his head against me, actually being calm for a change.

"You two look great together," she says. "I like your dog."

I'm about to tell her that Rowdy isn't my dog, but she keeps talking.

"I got Mickey when he was a puppy. He's twelve now, so he's getting up there." She lowers her voice. "When Mickey disappeared today I was so scared. I was afraid that..."

This woman looks like she's about to cry. She catches herself and changes the subject.

"Do you and your dog ever run in that?"

"In what?"

She points to a banner hanging on the bridge that leads across the river.

"*Pets In The Park*," I read. "No. Rowdy doesn't belong to me. And I'm not a runner."

"Too bad," she says. "Pets In The Park is a fundraiser for the Humane Society. Mickey and I did that run every year when he was younger. Last year we just walked the five miles. This year, Mickey has decided to pass on it altogether. Lots of people walk the course though. You just get some sponsors and go out and have fun with your dog. Or with someone else's dog. It's okay if you're not a runner."

A runner like Carly.

Then something clicks inside my head. I spring off the bench.

"Thanks for the idea! Bye, Mickey!"

The woman looks surprised. I don't stop to explain. After one last glance at the banner, Rowdy and I rush home.

chapter fourteen

An hour later I'm stepping out of the shower. I dress quickly and grab the papers from my desk. Then I head out the door.

As I ring Carly's doorbell, it occurs to me that this is either the best idea I've ever had, or the stupidest. When Matt answers the door I'm convinced it's the stupidest.

"Yeah?"

"Uh—is Carly here?"

"Yeah." He doesn't call her though.

"Can I talk to her?"

"What for?"

I'm trying to think of what to say when Carly steps into the room.

"Matt, who was that?" Then she sees me. "Oh. *You*."

The way Carly says it doesn't exactly raise my hopes.

"Can I talk to you, Carly?"

"You've got one minute. *One minute* and that's all." Carly plunks down on the couch. I look at Matt, who finally takes the hint and lumbers out of the room.

Then I look at Carly again. Her face is as dark as a thundercloud.

I've gotta come clean. Fast!

"Carly, I know I screwed up. Big time. And any reason I give you is just going to sound like a dumb excuse. So I'm not going to give a reason. And you were right last night—"

"When I said you were a jerk?"

"Uh, yeah."

This is going really well.

At that moment, Buddy comes into the room. He lopes over and licks my hand.

"Carly, I'm sorry. Especially 'cause you trusted me with Buddy."

Carly still says nothing. I pull the papers from my back pocket and shuffle through them.

I hold Carly's mom's check out. Carly's face darkens more when she sees what's in my hand.

"It's not like last night when I tried to give this back to you, Carly."

"Then what are you doing with it?"

"I'd like to use this money for something else. Not for my business, which, incidentally, I'm shutting down. But for this." I show Carly the forms for Pets In The Park.

"I'm not a runner like you. And I don't like to sweat." I try to ignore the trickle of sweat that is running down my neck. "Actually, I *hate* to sweat. But I'm going to do this anyway. It's a run in Hawrelak Park that people do with their dogs. It's to raise money for the Humane Society. I've already asked Mrs. Nielsen. She says that Rowdy can be my running partner. Or maybe my passing-out-from-exhaustion partner."

I'm not sure, but I think Carly smiles a little.

"I'd like to use your mom's check for my first sponsor. If that's okay with you and your mom, that is..."

Carly shrugs. "I could ask her, I guess."

"There's one more thing." I shuffle through the papers. "I downloaded an extra registration paper and pledge form. I was wondering, er...hoping actually, that you'd run this with me. You know, you and Buddy."

Carly looks down at Buddy. She doesn't say anything.

"That is, if you're interested. I'm gonna run it anyway—or try to. Rowdy might need to drag me most of the way, but I'm going to go for it," I say. "And I know you do really serious racing. So maybe this is too easy for you and you just don't want to."

Through all my babbling, I finally notice that Carly has said something.

"What was that?" I ask.

"I said I'll think about it."

"Thanks." I don't trust myself to say anything else.

I glance back quickly at Carly as I close her front door behind me. Then I realize I'm still holding her forms for Pets In The Park. I slip them into the mailbox.

None of the guys believe me when I tell them that I've shelved the business. Leo looks totally shell-shocked and doesn't say anything. But the other guys say lots!

"We were meeting the best girls of our lives!" Jonathan says.

"Yeah, the business was working for us!" Brad says.

"How are we gonna meet girls now?" Kyle asks.

"I don't know," I say. "But you'll have to try something new. Like maybe going up to them and saying hi or something."

"But what about all the dogs? And their owners?" Justin says.

"I'm going to call the dogs' owners and tell them I'm closing up shop. If they still want someone to walk their dogs, I'll give them the phone number of whoever walked their dog last. They can pay you directly.

But remember, you're just walking their dogs for the sake of walking their dogs. That's all."

"He's gone soft," Kyle says.

"Yeah, gone to the dogs," Justin agrees.

The guys slowly drift out the door. It's just me and Leo left now.

"You doing okay?" I ask.

"Yeah." Leo sighs. "I guess we should have seen this coming."

I nod.

"By the way," Leo says. "Did you talk to Carly yet?"

I tell him about going over to Carly's place and about the race.

"Running? *You*? The man who's—"

"Yeah, I know. The sweat thing. Carly and Buddy might run it with me."

"What are you thinking, Turk? I know Carly's into running. But, jeez, you said *you'd* do it too?"

"Yeah."

Leo shakes his head. "So when is this race?"

"The end of June."

"That's just a few weeks away. How far do you have to run?"

"Five miles."

Leo lets out his breath in a long, low whistle. "Are you gonna train?"

"I think I'd better."

"Well first, how about a hot chocolate on our way home? This could be our last before you have a heart attack during that race."

"Sure, Leo. I'll buy, okay?"

When I phone the dogs' owners, a lot of them say they want the guys to keep walking their dogs. But, as usual, that leaves me with Rowdy. So I end up doing what Ms. Kynsi told me to do way back in the beginning—starting small and doing the work myself.

And when it comes to Rowdy, the best way to burn all that energy is running. Plus it's good training for Pets In The Park, which is just two days away.

Leo has almost stopped rolling his eyes when I leave the school in my running shoes. This is a lot for him to wrap his mind around.

"There's still time to back out," he tells me Friday afternoon at my locker.

"Nope."

"Okay. I tried to warn you."

"Yeah, I know. Hey, do you have any spare cash?"

"A bit," Leo says. "Why? You up for a hot chocolate?"

"No. I've gotta run over and pick up Rowdy. But I was thinking I could use a few more sponsors for the race on the weekend."

Leo groans, but he signs my pledge form and hands over five dollars.

"Seriously Leo, about this running. I still don't understand why Carly's so hooked on it. But I'm starting to think I might finish the race without dying."

"Good for you. I still wouldn't risk it."

"Hey, I'm not looking forward to it either. But I'm in deep. I'll let you know how it goes."

"No," Leo shakes his head. "Spare me the gory details, okay?"

chapter fifteen

"You're up early today," Mom says. "And that's good, because I've been thinking."

This means trouble!

"We haven't had any quality family time for a while. That last time—when we had all the dogs—I'm not sure that really counts."

I cringe, remembering that night.

"So," Mom continues, "I was thinking maybe today—"

"Not today," I say. "You know that race you and Dad sponsored me for a while back?"

"Yes."

"It's this morning. Over at Hawrelak Park. Did you forget?"

Mom and Dad both jump. "No, of course not."

What would the parenting magazines say about that?

"But you could help. Rowdy and I need a lift over to the park."

Mom looks worried. She's probably picturing Rowdy bouncing around inside her Mercedes.

"Come on," I say. "It'll be fun. And I've really missed our family time lately..."

Mom pauses. I can almost hear the wheels turning in her head. And I can almost see the headline from her parenting magazine: *Learning to Meet Your Teen Halfway.*

"Well, uh, I guess we could give you a ride. Let's take *your* car, Mack."

Mom keeps glancing back at Rowdy and me as we drive to Hawrelak Park. I try to keep

Rowdy on the floor, but he jumps up on the backseat about a dozen times.

"Do you want us to stay?" Dad asks.

"No, it's okay."

The fewer people that see me puke or pass out during the race, the better!

I follow Dad's gaze over to the parking lot where some dogs are sniffing around the cars. One has just lifted his leg to pee on a tire. That's all that Dad needs to see before he's happy to beat it out of here.

"Okay then. Will you need a lift home?"

"No. I'll be fine."

"Have a good run," Mom says as I fumble out of the backseat with Rowdy.

I frantically look around for Carly and Buddy. There's no sign of either of them. There's just tons of dogs and tons of runners and tons of other people.

I notice that the runners have numbers pinned to their shirts. A guy with a German shepherd jogs past Rowdy and me.

"Hey! Where did you get the number for your shirt?"

"Over there." He points up ahead. "At the registration tent."

A man in an official-looking vest sees me. "You'd better get over there with your pledge form. The race is starting soon."

"Here, pin this on," the woman at the desk tells me. "Then hurry over to the start."

I'm looking around for Carly the whole time. No luck.

The next thing I know, Rowdy and I are jammed into the starting area with the rest of the dogs and runners. While Rowdy bounces beside me, I take one last desperate look for Carly. There's still no sign of her. Darn! I'd hoped she'd be here. That she might give me another chance. Not that I can blame her if she doesn't.

"*Go!*"

The clock starts and everyone takes off. Rowdy and I run with the crowd. Even though we've barely started, I'm already breathing hard. This can't be good!

Then suddenly, Carly and Buddy are beside us.

"Carly," I pant out. "You're here!"

She smiles. "Yeah. What did you think?"

"That I'd screwed up too bad," I gasp, "and that you weren't coming."

"Well, I'm here."

I'm so relieved that my knees nearly buckle underneath me.

A few minutes later, Carly asks, "How do you like your first race so far?"

"It's okay." I hope I don't look like I'm in too much pain. "Rowdy and I are probably running way too slow for you and Buddy. You can go on ahead if you want."

As I say this, I feel like I'm an early explorer, telling the rest of the crew to save themselves, and leave me here to die.

Then Carly smiles. "Okay. I'll just step it up a notch. See you at the finish line."

I watch as Carly's stride lengthens. Moments later she's moved up through the crowd with Buddy, and I can't even see her ponytail bobbing.

"Yeah, see you at the finish line," I say as I settle in for the long run ahead. "We'll get there too. Right, Rowdy?"